The Poor Little Owl

Betty and John are worried. Who will feed the baby owls now that their mother is gone?

Enid Blyton's
The Poor Little Owl

In the field nearby lived a little brown owl. John and Betty often saw it sitting on the telegraph wires in the dusk, when they went to bed.

"Tvit, tvit, tvit!" said the little owl to them, and the children called, "Tvit, tvit!" back to it. It wasn't very big, and when it spread its wings it flew very silently indeed.

Then one evening, as John and Betty walked home, they saw the little owl disappear into a hole in an old, old willow tree. "I guess it has got its nest there!" said John in excitement. "I wonder if there will be any baby owls? We must watch and see."

But before they knew, a sad thing happened to the little owl. It went to drink from the pond one night, overbalanced, fell into the water and couldn't get out! So in the morning John and Betty found that it was drowned, and they were very sad.

"Oh John—what about the baby owls, if there are any in the tree?" said Betty in tears. "There won't be anyone to feed them. They will starve to death, poor things."

John spoke to the gardener about the nest he was sure was in the old willow tree. "Couldn't you look and see if there are any baby owls there?" he said. "We don't want them to starve, you know."

"I'm not going after any owls," said the gardener at once. "Dangerous creatures they are, with their sharp claws! My goodness, even a baby owl can get its claws into you so hard that you can't get them out. Torn to pieces your hand would be!"

"Oh," said John. He went away, but he kept on and on thinking about the owls. He felt sure they were hungry and unhappy. "Betty, there must be *some* way of getting them out," he said. "Do think. You're clever at thinking."

So Betty thought. "Well," she said, "if their claws are so sharp and strong that they can dig right into your hand and not let it go, what about letting down something into the nest—a handkerchief, perhaps—and letting them dig their claws into that. Then all we need to do is to draw up the handkerchief and the owls will come too!"

"Marvellous idea!" cried John. And so it was. Betty borrowed a big old silk hanky from Daddy's drawer, and the two children went to the old willow tree. They climbed up it and came to the hole, which went deep into a thick branch of the tree.

A faint hissing noise came up from the hole. "Goodness—is there a snake in there?" said Betty.

"No! Owls do hiss, you know," said John. "Now, Betty—where's the hanky? Hand it over."

John took the hanky and let one end slowly down the hole. There were two baby owls in the tree. They turned themselves over so that their clawed feet were on top—and how they attacked that silk hanky! They dug their feet into it and their claws caught in the silk.

"Got them nicely!" shouted John, and he pulled up the hanky. There were the two fluffy baby owls holding on to it for all they were worth! John popped them into a box he had brought with him, shut the lid, and then switched his torch on to see the nest.

"There isn't really any nest," he called to Betty, "just a few shavings from the hole, that's all. But wait a minute—what's this?"

The light of his torch had shone on to something red. John put his hand into the hole and felt what it was. It seemed to be a little bag of some sort. He pulled at it—and it came out. It was heavy.

"Betty! The owl had made her nest on top of this little bag!" cried John. "Look—it's got the name of the bank on it. I do believe it's the bag of money that a thief stole from the bank messenger last winter! He must have hidden it here and then forgotten where the hiding place was!"

"Goodness!" said Betty, as John opened the little red bag and a whole heap of shining golden coins winked up at them. "What a lot of money! Come and tell Mother."

Well, that was a most exciting afternoon. The children had two baby owls to look after, and a bag of money to give back to the bank! And what do you think? The bank manager gave the children one of the coins! "That's your reward," he said. "Buy what you like with it."

So what do you think they bought with the money? They went to the shops and bought a marvellous cage in which to bring up their two baby owls! It was painted blue outside, and had red perches inside, and was very grand and big indeed.

"You can keep your little owls there and bring them up in safety till they are big enough to fly away and look after themselves," said Mother. "You must feed them well, give them fresh water, and clean out their cage every single day."

So they did, and soon the two owls grew tame and friendly, and sat peacefully on the children's fingers whenever they were held out to them. Betty and John were very proud of their owls, because no one else at school had owls; and even the teacher came to see them, and said what strange and curious birds they were.

"They look rather like little feathered cats!" she said. And so they did, as they sat side by side on their perches, their big golden eyes looking solemnly at the visitor.

And now they have flown away to look after themselves; but John and Betty have left the cage door open in case they might like to come back there to sleep. I expect they will sometimes.

Every night the two little birds call to their friends and say, "Tvit, tvit, tvit!" from the nearby field. I wonder if *you* have heard them. They call so sharply and so loudly that I shouldn't be a bit surprised if you hear them too!